Debbie Macomber & Mary Lou Carney

The Truly Terribly Horrible Sweater ...That Grandma Knit

Pictures by Vincent Nguyen

HARPER
An Imprint of HarperCollinsPublishers

*O*nly three more days until my birthday, Cameron Girard thought as he raced in the door from soccer practice and kicked off his cleats. That's when he saw it: Grandma Susan's present had come in the mail!

Cameron picked up the package and shook it.

What could it be?

A new video game?

A remote control car?

Maybe it was a cool blinking light for his bicycle!

Cameron could hardly wait to open his birthday present from his grandma Susan. She always gave the best gifts!

Finally, the day arrived.

Cameron flew out of bed and down to the kitchen, where his mother and father and baby sister were waiting for him.

On his plate was a big stack of pancakes with candles sticking out the top. *I wish this would be my best birthday ever!* He closed his eyes and blew out the candles in one big breath.

"Can I open Grandma Susan's present now?"

"If that's what you want!" Mom said.

Cameron tore off the paper and opened the box. A yellow envelope lay on top of the tissue paper.

"Read the card first," Mom told him.

Inside was Grandma Susan's note:

This is a very special gift for a very special boy. Happy birthday!

Holding his breath, Cameron opened the box.

It wasn't a video game.

It wasn't a remote control car.

It wasn't a blinking light for his bike.

It was a *sweater*.

A truly terribly horrible sweater.

"Oh, Cameron!" his mother said. "Look what Grandma knit for you! It's almost like the one she made for your baby sister."

Cameron did *not* want a sweater for his birthday—even if his grandma Susan had knitted it.

His mother held it up for him to see. It had red, green, yellow, blue, and orange stripes. Even worse, it had big buttons.

If his friends saw him wear this, they would laugh.

It was a truly terribly horrible sweater . . . and Cameron was never ever going to wear it.

The next day Cameron called his dog, Scout, into his bedroom and closed the door. Carefully he slipped Scout's front legs into the sleeves of his birthday sweater and buttoned the rest around Scout's middle. It had rained all night, and Scout loved rolling in the puddles. "I'll never have to wear his sweater now," Cameron whispered to his dog.

On Cameron's way out the door, his dad stopped him. "Whoa, Cameron!" he said. "Isn't that your new sweater? It's to keep *you* warm, not Scout. Besides, the backyard is a muddy mess!"

Slowly Cameron took the sweater off Scout.

Then, one chilly morning a few weeks later, as his mother was making his lunch, she said, "This would be a perfect day to wear your new sweater to school."

Cameron went in his room and pulled out the sweater. He buttoned the big buttons. But . . .

It was a truly terribly horrible sweater . . . and Cameron was never ever going to wear it.

So before he even reached the bus stop, Cameron stuffed his
birthday gift into his backpack, where none of his friends would see it.

Just before Thanksgiving, Cameron had another chance to get rid of the sweater.

"I'm running some things down to the church for their rummage sale!" Mom called to him. "Cameron, is there anything you want to donate?"

Cameron had an idea.

"Yes!" he shouted back. He grabbed the sweater, bolted down the stairs, and raced out to the car. "Here, Mom!" he said, and tossed his bundle into the trunk.

His mom pulled out of the driveway, and Cameron smiled. That birthday sweater was gone for good.

But when Mother came home, she was carrying the sweater. "Look what I found mixed in with the rummage sale stuff. Thank goodness I saw it in time!" Dragging his feet, Cameron carried the sweater to his room. He buried it in the bottom of his closet next to his bike helmet.

It was a truly terribly horrible sweater . . . and Cameron was never ever going to wear it.

Cameron knew his mom would find the sweater eventually, so he came up with another idea. One night, when everyone was asleep, he sneaked down to the kitchen, carrying the sweater. He spread it out carefully and opened the refrigerator.

Take this, sweater!

He squirted rivers of red ketchup, then added globs of goopy mustard. Finally, he scooped on piles of slimy mayonnaise. Then he tossed the sweater into the laundry basket.

The next morning, as his mother was leaving for the grocery store, he heard a shriek.

"CAMERON!" his mother yelled. "What happened to your sweater?"

"Oh," Cameron said, trying not to smile. "I got hungry last night and made myself a snack."

"Your special sweater is a mess," his mother told him.

"Sorry, Mom," Cameron said. And he *was* sorry. Sorry he didn't like the sweater. Sorry that Grandma Susan had gone to so much trouble to knit him such a truly terribly horrible birthday gift.

That night at dinner, the sweater was folded and lying on his chair. "Every single stain came out!" Mom said happily. "Grandma Susan would have been heartbroken if anything happened to this sweater."

Baby Mia giggled and smashed peas into her hair.

Cameron hadn't thought about that. He didn't want to make Grandma sad.

Still, it was a truly terribly horrible sweater . . . and Cameron was never ever going to wear it.

In December, as Cameron was helping his dad with the Christmas decorations, his mother told him the news. "Grandma Susan is coming. She'll be here Saturday and stay with us until after Christmas. We're all going to the train station to pick her up." Mom looked directly at him. "And Cameron, she will want to see you wearing your sweater."

Cameron was excited to see his grandma Susan. She liked the same board games he did, and she let him read to her. Plus she clapped really loudly when she watched him shoot hoops in the driveway. It would almost be worth wearing the truly terrible sweater just to be with her. So he put the sweater on when they went to pick her up at the train station.

"Hello, hello!" Grandma waved as she spotted them.

"Grandma! Grandma!" Cameron yelled, and raced to meet her.

Grandma Susan bent down and pulled him close. "I'm so glad you like your sweater. You look so handsome in it!"

Cameron frowned as he stared down at the bright stripes and big buttons. How could he look handsome wearing a truly terribly horrible sweater?

The next morning, Grandma came into Cameron's room. The sweater was lying on the floor next to Scout. She picked it up and sat on the bed beside Cameron, spreading the sweater across his bedspread. "Let me tell you about knitting this sweater for you," she said.

Her finger traced the green stripe. "As I knit these rows, I imagined I was at one of your soccer games, watching you race across the grass. I remembered the time I saw you play. You kicked in the winning goal and everyone cheered."

Cameron smiled. "No one cheered louder than you, Grandma."

"And look at the blue ripple here. I chose that color because it's the same as your bicycle. Remember last summer when your dad took off the training wheels? You were scared, but you pedaled all by yourself down the street for half a block. Then you phoned to tell me all about it.

"Blue reminded me that you are going to go far in life."

Cameron looked up at his grandmother.

"Can you guess why I used the orange yarn?" Grandma Susan asked.

Cameron laughed. He knew why. "'Cause I love oranges so much."

His grandma nodded. "I have never seen a little boy who ate more oranges than you."

"What about the yellow?" he asked.

His grandma put her arm around his shoulder. "Yellow is the happiest color I know. I remember the day your mom and dad called to tell me they had a baby boy. They were so excited and happy! Your mom and dad waited a long time to have a baby. It didn't seem it would ever happen—and then you were born. You, Cameron, are the sunshine of *all* our lives."

Cameron hugged his grandma tight.

"Red, of course, is the color of hearts," Grandma said. "And you are always close to my heart, even when we're far apart."

As Grandma bent to kiss the top of his head, Cameron looked again at the sweater she had knit him. He thought about the hours Grandma had spent choosing yarn and then knitting. This birthday present was one of a kind. Special, just like his grandma.

Suddenly the sweater didn't look truly, terribly horrible anymore.

It looked good. It looked like something Cameron would be proud to wear.

For a very long time.

HOW TO KNIT

Ask an experienced knitter (maybe your grandmother!) to cast on 20 stitches for you.

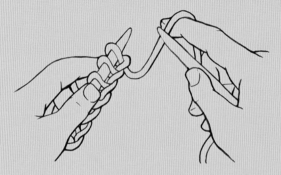

Then take the knitting needles into your own hands. The empty needle should be in your right hand. The needle with the stitches should be in your left hand. There will be a long "tail" of yarn hanging from the left-hand needle.

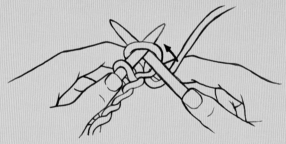

Take the point of the right-hand needle and slip it into the first loop on the left-hand needle, moving the right needle underneath the left needle.

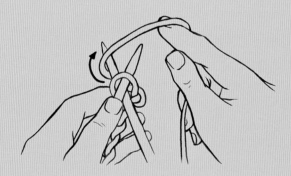

Take the loose yarn in your right hand. Wrap the yarn around the tip of the right-hand needle. Make sure you go counterclockwise.

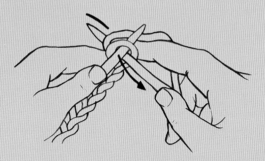

Now for the tricky part: Pull the tip of the right-hand needle through the loop on the left-hand needle. Go from back to front.

Slip the stitch you have made off the left-hand needle onto the right-hand needle.

You're done! You've made a stitch!

Keep doing the same thing for the next nineteen stitches, then turn your needles around and start again. You're knitting! Soon you'll be an experienced knitter, too.

THE TRULY TERRIBLY WONDERFUL SWEATER

For experienced knitters

Materials:

1 skein each of 6 colors or a variety of leftover worsted-weight yarns

24" circular ndl & dpn size 6 or size that gives you your gauge

markers, tapestry needles, scrap yarn

Sizes: 6 yrs (8 yrs, 10 yrs), 28" (29½", 31")

Gauge: 19 sts/4 inches in stockinette stitch

Colors we used: #1 green, #2 red, #3 turquoise, #4 orange, #5 yellow, #6 navy

Abbreviations:

K – knit

P – purl

co – cast on

inc – increase

sts – stitches

RS – right side

rnds – rounds

WS – wrong side

BO – bind off

pu&k – pick up & knit

ndl – needle

dpn – double point needles

K2tog – knit 2 together

SSK – slip, slip, knit

pm – place marker

Directions:

W/circular needle and color #1 co 118(130,134) sts and work K2,P2 rib for 2½ inches. Begin color pattern and inc 12 sts for all sizes evenly spaced across in first row. Work even in color pattern for 10½(12,13) inches.

Divide for armholes: w/RS facing, work 32(35,36) sts in color pattern. Continue on these sts for 4(4,5) inches from armhole division.

Begin neck shaping: w/RS facing, BO 7(8,10) sts, work in pattern to end.

Next row (WS): work even in pattern.

Next row (RS): BO2, work even in pattern to end.

Next row (WS): work even in pattern.

Next row (RS): BO 1 st, work even in pattern to end.

Repeat the last 2 rows 4(5,7) more times.

Then work even in stripe pattern rows 111–122 till armhole measures 6(6½, 7) inches or desired length to shoulder. Place sts on scrap yarn.

Back: work even in color pattern on center back 66(72,74) sts till back measures same as right front. Place sts on scrap yarn.

Left front: on remaining 32(35,36) sts work even in color pattern till front measures 4(4,5) inches. Repeat neck shaping but work bind offs on WS rows, reversing shaping. Then work even till front is same length as right front & back.

Seam shoulders: place corresponding left back shoulder sts onto dpn and graft left front sts using same yarn color sts are. Place right front & back shoulder sts onto dpns and graft them. Leave back center neck sts on scrap yarn.

Sleeves: w/dpns and color #2 pick up & knit 58(62,66) sts around armhole, pm. Work in color pattern substituting color 1 for color 2 in Rows 11–26 , color 4 for color 3 in Rows 37–56, and color 2 for 1 more repeat of double moss stitch rows.

Work even in pattern for 3". Then begin sleeve shaping.

Next rnd: K1, K2tog, work to last 3 sts SSK, K1.

Work 4 rounds even.

Repeat these 5 rounds 6(7,8) times.

Then work even till sleeve measures 9(10,12) inches or 2" less than total desired length. If you need to add

. . . THAT GRANDMA KNIT

Designed by Susan DeRosa
of Amazing Threads

more length, you can include a section of double moss stitch as for Rows 11–26 in color pattern or garter stripes to desired length to cuff.

Work sleeve cuff in color #1 w/ K2,P2 rib (decreasing any sts you may need to attain a st count divisible by 4) for 2". BO.

Front bands:
Button band: (right side for boys, left side for girls):
w/24" circ ndl and color #1 pu&k 2 sts for every 2 rows along front. Work K2,P2 rib for 1¼". BO.
Buttonhole band: work as above but place buttonhole every 2" on center row of band.

Collar: w/color #1 pu&k 2 sts for every 3 rows along right front neck. Place back neck sts onto other end of circ ndl & K across them. Pu&k same # of sts you picked up along right front along left front. Knit 6 rows. BO. Weave in ends. Sew on buttons.

Color Pattern

1-green, 2-red, 3-turquoise, 4-orange, 5-yellow, 6-navy
Rows 1&2: w/color 2 K
Rows 3&4: w/color 3 K
Rows 5&6: w/color 5 K
Rows 7&8: w/color 6 K
Row 9&10 w/color 4 K
Row 11: w/2 K(rows 11-26 are worked w/color 2 in double moss st)
Row 12: k2,p2 across
Row 13: work sts as they appear
Row 14: p2,k2 across
Row 15: work sts as they appear
Rows 16-23: rep rows 12-15 2X
Rows 24&25: rep rows 12&13
Row 26: w/2 P
Rows 27&28: w/4 K

Rows 29&30: w/3 K
Rows 31&32: w/5 K
Rows 33&34: w/6 K
Rows 35&36: w/1 K
Row 37: w/3 K (Rows 37-56 are worked w/color 3 in seed stitch)
Row 38: w/3 K1,P1 across
Rows 39-56: w/3 K the P's & P the K's
Row 57&58: w/1 K
Rows 59&60: w/2 K
Rows 61&62: w/5 K
Rows 63&64: w/6 K
Rows 65&66: w/3 K
Row 67: w/5 K, this begins the simple seed st section. Rows 67-98 will be worked w/color 5.
Row 68: P
Row 69: K2 * P1, K3 rep from * across
Row 70: P
Row 71: K
Row 72: P
Row 73: K4 * P1, K3 rep from *across
Row 74: P
Repeat Rows 67-74 1X more
Row 83: K
Row 84: P
Rows 85&86: w/3 K
Rows 87&88: w/4 K
Rows 89&90: w/6 K
Rows 91&92: w/2 K
Rows 93&94: w/1 K
Rows 95-110: Repeat rows 85-94 till sweater measures desired length to shoulder.
Rows 111&112: w/1 K
Rows 113&114: w/2 K
Rows 115&116: w/5 K
Rows 117&118: w/3 K
Rows 119&120: w/6 K
Rows 121&122: w/4 k

To my grandson Cameron LaCombe, who inspired the story.
Not to worry, Cam. I'm knitting you socks next time.
—D.M.

To my sister Libby—the *real* knitter in our family
—M.L.C.

This book is for my three lovely sisters,
Theresa, Cassandra, and Veronica Nguyen.
—V.N.

The Truly Terribly Horrible Sweater . . . That Grandma Knit
Text copyright © 2009 by Debbie Macomber and Mary Lou Carney
Illustrations copyright © 2009 by Vincent Nguyen

Manufactured in China.
Library of Congress Cataloging-in-Publication Data is available.
ISBN 978-0-06-165093-2 (trade bdg.)

Typography by Rachel Zegar
❖
09 10 11 12 13 SCP 10 9 8 7 6 5 4 3 2 1
First Edition